CILIE YACK IS UNDER ATTACK!

This is the story of how one boy
turned his problems into a triumph

WRITTEN AND ILLUSTRATED BY CARYN TALTY

Copyright 2010 by Caryn Talty

ISBN: 978-0-9828173-0-8 (paperback)
Library of Congress Control Number: 2010934916

Summary: Cilie, a 9 year old boy from Ireland, has many misadventures before his family learns he has celiac sprue. To everyone's surprise, this funny character with a penchant for cakes becomes quite a famous gluten-free chef.

Book design cover by Caryn Talty

Printed and bound in U.S.A.

MAP OF
COUNTY CLARE

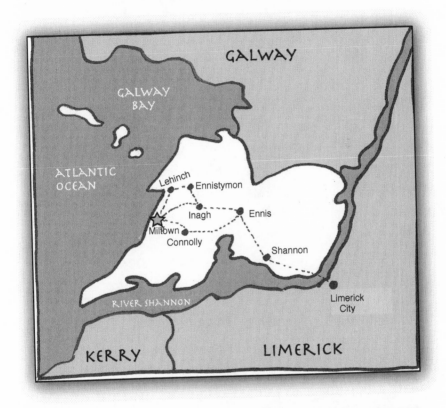

The little star on the map is Cilie's home town. It's called Miltown Malbay but the folks around there just call it Miltown for short. Most of Clare is surrounded by the Atlantic Ocean, the Galway Bay, and the River Shannon. The three ovals between the ocean and the bay are the Aran Islands. The dotted lines are the roads that Cilie travels on from place to place in the story.

A SPECIAL FORWARD FROM

"Celiac disease is an autoimmune disorder that affects just under 1 in 133 people in the United States. In adults, the symptoms can range from chronic diarrhea, abdominal pain, and rashes to less typical symptoms such as arthritis, infertility, and thyroid problems.

In children, however, the signs and symptoms of celiac disease may be severe, but are often more subtle. Children with celiac disease often have various gastrointestinal complaints, but as this story shows, often those complaints are not specific. Children with celiac disease may also present with slow growth and decreased weight gain, but often, due to the lack of experience the health care professionals have in diagnosing celiac disease, many of these children will remain undiagnosed for years.

Once diagnosed, a strict gluten-free diet is the only treatment for celiac disease. However, this treatment carries a large burden for both the patient and the patient's family. Celiac children are touched by this disease on many levels. Medical problems before and after the diagnosis, lifestyle changes after the diagnosis, and social pressures from school and friends all weigh upon the minds of children with celiac disease.

Cilie Yack is Under Attack is an entertaining story of one young Irish lad's journey through life before and after the diagnosis of celiac disease. Early on, Cilie, the main

DR. MICHELLE L. SULLIVAN, DO

character, really does not like to eat because of how poorly he feels afterward. The story walks the reader through the symptoms that children can face, the emotions involved in the diagnosis of celiac disease, and how overwhelming the start of a gluten-free lifestyle can be -- all as told from the perspective of a 9 year-old boy. We see Cilie try to tackle learning how to cook and bake gluten-free and follow him until this becomes second nature to both him and his family.

Cilie Yack is Under Attack is an inspirational work to all of those children and their families who are either undergoing testing for, or have been recently diagnosed with celiac disease. It shows that even our youngest patients are resilient enough to move forward. We all can learn a lot from young Cilie!"

Dr. Michelle L. Sullivan

Dr. Michelle Sullivan, D.O. P.C., is a board certified doctor with over 14 years in practice. She graduated from New York College of Osteopathic Medicine in 1993 and completed her residency at MacNeal Hospital in Berwyn, IL. in 1996. Today Dr. Sullivan lives with her husband and four children in the Chicago area. Dr. Sullivan has celiac disease herself and she successfully cares for many celiac patients in her practice. She understands the nuances of childhood celiac first hand because two of her children are diagnosed with it.

Dedications and Appreciations....

I want to dedicate this book to my family, especially my husband Noel. Thanks for your understanding and encouragement throughout the creative process. Thanks to Theresa, my diagnosed aunt and cooking partner. I have truly enjoyed all the time we have spent together in the kitchen. Thanks to all of my dear friends who've tasted our family's many gluten-free recipes over the years. Your encouragement and love has truly been felt. Thanks Mom and Dad for all your support, and to Ann and Pat, Marie, Jamie, Sean, Lourda, Paul, Saorise, Trish, John, and Michael- thank you for the inspiration. Even if we can't be with you in Ireland, know that Cilie lives with us in our hearts the same way that you do.

> And thanks to all my readers for believing in me!

I also dedicate this book to the many children in today's world who have been blessed with food intolerances at a young age and as a result have been forced to look at the unhealthy way our modern world eats. I say blessed because you have developed a maturity that far surpasses your peers. Boys and girls, be amazed and know that you have been given a gift. After you have given up these damaging foods you will feel your body go from sickness to health.

This will be a triumph that will make you very proud. You have to learn to avoid non-nutritious foods, but you have opened a world of possibility and imagination in your new allergy-free kitchen. A healthy lifestyle has become part of your everyday world. You think about food, what it can do to you, how it can heal your body, and how a little bit of creativity can make magic happen when you are cooking.

Finally, I would like to especially dedicate this book to my three sons. Without our family's forced food intolerance journey and my sons' love for cooking there would be no Cilie. Ian, Conor, and Ryan have been my inspiration from the very beginning. My boys are charming characters and it just seemed so fitting to create a character that has a little bit of each boy's personality in him. I have watched my boys as they have learned to navigate a food-filled world on a restricted diet, and although the road has been bumpy at times, overall it has been so very, very, good.

Cilie, too, has a similar journey and story to tell. Enjoy the humor, but more especially understand that Cilie's feelings about his restricted diet are universal. If you have food allergies and are on a special diet like Cilie's, know that you are not alone. There are so many boys and girls just like you all over the world.

I truly hope you enjoy getting to know our dear beloved Cilie, whom I've grown to love very much and hope that you do too.

Enjoy the story.

With Warmest Regards,

Caryn Talty

CILIE YACK IS UNDER ATTACK!

This is the story of how one boy
turned his problems into a triumph,
and how you can too!

Do you see the word Fáilte written above my door? Fáilte is a Gaelic word that means 'welcome' in Ireland. It sounds like 'FALL-t-cha' when you say it.

Table of Contents....

Chapter 1

I'M CILIE, NOT "SILLY," SILLY!

Hi, My name is Cilie Yack. It is a Gaelic name and it sounds like "silly" when you say it. My mum says it means "from the narrow channel." She likes that it is unique. You see, Mum's an artist. So she is a bit different than other mums. For one thing, she doesn't get mad when we draw on the walls in our bedroom. We have all kinds of paintings, charcoal bits, canvases, brushes, and pencils all around our house. Mum likes when things are a bit off center. She likes when life is a bit more colorful around the edges. If she had been able to look into a crystal ball the day I was born I think she would have been surprised. My life has turned out to be

This is me by the Glendine river with my dog Buddy. He goes everywhere around the fields with me. His job is to help Dad move the cattle. My job is to count them.

pretty colorful and off center so far. It is just the way she likes it. And do you know what? I like it too.

I'm a really funny kid. Everybody I know thinks my name suits me down to the ground. When I was younger 'Cilie' just meant 'silly' to everybody that knew me. It used to bother me that no one noticed the real me underneath all those silly jokes I said and funny noises I made. Some kids used to tease me a lot when I was small. After a while I learned to handle it by doing even more funny stuff to get a laugh.

13

I made a reputation for myself, so I did.

That was Dad's idea, actually- being funny when your getting teased. He's much different than Mum. Mum is particular about details, and if they are not just perfect you'd better look out. Dad just takes everything 'handy' all the time. Do you know what that means? He just rolls right along every day and only worries when it counts.

When I was younger school was hard. I would always imagine things in my head during the school day. It made me forget myself. Sometimes I would forget to ask before going to the toilet. Other times I would forget to take my folder out and put it on my desk. I was pretty bad at paying attention during lessons. I also had problems staying in the lines, too. My hands just never wanted to do what they were told.

14

It didn't matter how hard I tried. My brain was always racing ahead to the next thing. It hardly had time to do what was expected. So I got teased a lot.

Dad says that nobody picks on the comedian. They all want to be around him for a good laugh. If you get picked on a lot you should listen to his advice. You know what? It's true. I'm living proof that his idea works.

When I was six I already had my bad reputation with the teachers at my school. They thought that I was a real prankster. It is one of the bad side effects of being funny.

Dad keeps warning me all the time about being funny during class. I *do* listen to him more now than I did when I was younger. But sometimes I get a really funny idea and I can't help myself.

I had one of those ideas last year. I was bored in class one afternoon and my mind just started wandering all over the place. The class was supposed to be coloring maps of Ireland and labeling all the waterways. I had a lint covered raisin stuck in my pocket that I was toying with. It was just dying to get out of there. I fought the urge for a long time. Finally, I just couldn't help it. I pulled him out and started playing with my newly named 'Mr. Raisin man' on the table.

"Meet Mr. Raisin man," I said in my best super-

hero voice. That caught everyone's attention.

"He can lift heavy pencils. Weeeee. He can lift a ruler. Grrrrrrr. He can lift a book. Uggghhhh...."

I was on a roll. All the lads around me were laughing. Then one of the lads wondered if Mr. Raisin could fly. By the way, that was when I should have quit.

But I didn't. The next thing I knew the lads and I had a plan. I gave Mr. Raisin a running start. Then I threw him at the fan. I thought he would bounce off of the blade and back. Boys and girls, I'm telling you, don't try this at home. Mr. Raisin man definitely doesn't fly. He just gets stuck to the fan blade and goes *splat*.

Of course the lads were roaring loudly at my stupidity. I had done it again. I performed successful comedy at no charge, but it was at my own expense. My reward was a week of indoor study. I think in America you call it detention. Dad and Mum weren't pleased. I had to shovel the stalls by myself after that. You know, I'm not all bad. I really try hard to stay in line most times,

especially now. This year I have Mrs. Murphy for a teacher. She has a third eye in the back of her head glued to my every move. She tells me that all the time. She's on my case because she knows I'm a prankster. She is tough but nice. When someone does something bad behind her back she will look at me first. I know that sounds unfair, but you should know a few things:

1. *I definitely earned my reputation.*
2. *I come from a small village and you pretty much know everyone by the time you are 2 years old.*
3. *Did I mention that I earned it?*

17

But about five months ago I became a celebrity around here, and it wasn't for my funny bone. I've really started to change. I don't need to be funny for attention now. I actually found out I'm good at something besides jokes. By the way, I'm 9, in case you were wondering. I'm in third class now, which is about the same as being in fourth grade in America. I have cousins in America. They are always so confused about things that just seem so normal to me in Ireland.

I will be 10 after the holidays and I can't wait. Mum said she is going to take me to see a movie

Lately I find myself looking over my shoulder every time one of the lads so much as cracks a joke.

without my little brothers tagging along. If you have brothers then you know why that is such a great present. They have a kids' club on Saturdays. I'm not sure what I want to see yet. The holidays are still a long way off so I have loads of time to figure it out. It will probably be something funny and not scary, though. Mum hates scary movies.

I know she's taking me because she is really proud of me all around. This year is the first year Mum got to miss all those after school chats with the teacher. You see, I really am slowly changing my reputation. It feels good to be on the other side of trouble for a change. But Mrs. Murphy is still watching me like a hawk. She says it is her duty to keep me on the straight and narrow, especially now that I've gotten some notice.

I probably have you wondering. So how did I go from a stand up comic and classroom troublemaker to a totally upstanding kid?

Well, I'll tell you.

It is simple.

I found my niche. (By the way, in case you are wondering how to say that, it sounds like **'nitch'**).

You know what niche means, right? I found that one thing that I am really, really good at. Yes, after all this time I finally did....

Chapter 2

FAMILY BUSINESS

We have a big family and there are a lot of boys in it. This comes in very handy because we own a pretty big dairy farm. My Dad has two brothers; Granddad has two brothers, and most of my cousins happen to be boys. Oh, and I have two younger brothers too. But I think their names are an improvement from Cilie. I have one brother who's seven-and-a-half. He's Desmond but everyone just calls him Dessie. It really sounds like 'Dezzie' when the Irish say it, so try to remember that when you are reading my story.

My youngest brother is Ronan. He's six. If you ask me, he gets away with everything around here. When he was three Dad said Ronan was born with two

This is Dessie shoveling slurry. We have to clean the slurry out of the sheds every night. Slurry is cow poop, by the way. We put it on the fields to make the grass grow better.

---

long legs and no ears. Dad's only kidding about having no ears. Ronan actually has pretty big ears like me. Dad really means that my brother ran off all the time and didn't listen when he was told 'no'. He still doesn't like when my parents tell him 'no' but at least they don't have to key lock the front door anymore. We used to do that so he wouldn't escape out of the house. One morning when he was two he wound up in the milking shed.

So that is how the long legs legend came about. Ronan had enough sense to put on a pair Dad's rubber boots. They reached all the way up to his waist. Mum had no idea how he managed to walk without bending his knees. The milking shed isn't far. It is only at the top of the road from our house. But for a two-year-old with boots up to his waist it's like climbing a mountain.

I'm sure you can imagine all the many conversations I've had with Dad about the fine job they did picking my name. They set me up for a lifetime of pranks and practical jokes. He once said to me, "If you don't like your given name then become a priest."

My Dad is quite the comedian. He's right up there with Brendan Grace on television. He told me in private that Mum picked my name and he just agreed to it to keep the peace. He said Mum really wanted a name that was traditional and unique. He said I shouldn't complain. He said she almost named me Teagan. That probably doesn't mean much to my American cousins, but here in Ireland it's also a girl's name. So I guess I'd rather be silly then be a sissy.

Our cows need milking twice a day no matter what. If Dad can't milk them in the evening we have to get Granddad to come over. That's Long Legs Ronan there in front when he was 2 years old.

My cousin Sean was born a week before me. I am fully aware that I could have gotten his name if I had been born a little sooner. Oh, don't worry. I never let him live THAT down.

So this is my story about my life. You are probably wondering why on earth a kid who's only 9 is writing a book about his life. Well, I guess you could say it's because I'm sort of a celebrity these days in my hometown.

Actually, I'm a celebrity in all of Co. Clare. I even got a quick mention on RTE radio news one afternoon. Granddad was over the moon about it. He told me so himself.

Whoa, did I hear that right? Whoops! My toast!!!!

I'm told I'm not to brag about it, though. Mum says, "Self praise is no praise." So I am supposed to keep that sort of thing to myself. But I know that she and Dad are just as proud as

Granddad. They just don't want me to get a big head about it.

So if you ever run into her at the store in Miltown, say nothing. Don't tell her you heard me talking about myself like that. Whatever you do, don't mention anything about me. Don't ask about that big contest I won. You know the one at the South Court Hotel in Limerick City?

Well, I actually never went to the South Court where the original contest was held. I just went out to dinner with Mum and Nana one afternoon at the West County. It is in nearby Ennis. Then I did something I still can't believe I had the nerve to do. But I won't spoil the surprise by telling you just yet.

You must be wondering how a hotel owner like Niall Lynch would not only listen to me, but let me prove myself. But he didn't stop there. He turned me into a celebrity at the end of it all.

So all I can say is that you better go to the toilet right now before you get too caught up in my story. There is a lot to tell. I am sure you are not going to want to put this story down until it is finished.

Because I know that your time is important I will skip right over my baby years and get to the juicy stuff.

Besides I don't remember that stuff anyway. Only Mum and Dad do.

I will just get to the point about my problem. I was born with a magical gene that makes wheat some kind of poison for me and it practically blows up my intestines on impact. Okay, not really. I am exaggerating a bit here. You sort of have to forgive me. I like science a lot and I read a lot of books all the time. I was just trying to be funny. Which reminds me, Mum says that I need to know my audience. So I better be a little more clear. I was diagnosed a few years ago with a thing they call celiac sprue. It sounds pretty serious, and trust me it is, but I am not going to die or anything from it. I'm perfectly healthy and fine now. Actually, I've never felt better in my life.

But back then....

Hey, did you know that in Ireland school starts at 9:00 am? We also go to school until the very end of June. Religion classes and uniforms are mandatory here. I have to wear a tie every single day. Kids in Ireland don't get hot lunches either. We bring our own.

Chapter 3

THE START OF THE PROBLEM

My first memory of school was quite an experience for me and Mum.

I was just about 3 1/2 years old. I was quite a handful, as the legend of me would have it. Mum had taken me down to visit the junior infants class. It is the same thing as being in kindergarten in America, only we start when we are 4. The school is called St. Joseph's and it is in Spanish Point. We went on a cold spring day. Dessie was still a baby. Mum was also just about ready to have my baby brother Ronan.

Dad says she wanted to get me out of her hair. Mum says that is ridiculous. She wanted no such thing. She said that I loved books from an early age. She

Bump, Bump, Bump.... Mum held on tight to the pram while little Dessie tried hard not to fall out.

---

thought the junior infants class was going to be fantastic for my developing mind. She said it would prepare me for national school. So we went for a tour that day. It started out as a thoughtful and intelligent idea on Mum's part. But it quickly turned into a nightmare for both of us.

We arrived during the middle of the day. I was pretty impatient waiting for her to maneuver my chubby baby brother around in the pram. She drove slowly over those bumps and steps in the walkway and the entrance. That big baby pram had such tiny wheels and they managed to get caught on everything.

29

I met the principal and got to see the classroom first hand. I was feeling like a king. The place was huge but that didn't scare me at all. There were loads of kids in there and I'm sure a teacher too. But I wasn't really focused on all that. I had never seen so many toys in all my life as I did in that room. So I did what any kid my age would do. I tore into the place to try it all out. Mum had to drag me out of there. I made a pretty big mess, so I'm told. I didn't like leaving, so I did what any normal three year old would in a situation like that. I started to cry and kick up. Well, that only frustrated poor Mummy. She took me to the office to fill out the papers and of course I decided not to wait for her to finish. I headed right back to the toy room. The principal left the office to help Mum find me.

They found me all right. And I wasn't budging. So Mrs. Lanigan, the principal, offered me a cookie. It was a lovely thin biscuit with chocolate on top. Dad used to dip those ones in his tea cup until they were really soggy. Then he would pop them in his mouth and chew.

Does Cilie want a biscuit?

30

Well I took the bait, you could say. It was a long walk from that fine class back to the office. I must have eaten half the package. Mum finished up her meeting and when it was time to go I decided she could leave without me. I became a right good hooligan. I flat out refused to leave with her.

"Come on Cilie," Mum said. "It's time to go home."

"No!"

"Cilie--"

"No. I want to go to school."

"You will, Cilie. Just not until September."

"No!"

The next part is fuzzy for me. Not for Mum, though. She gladly reminds me about what happened next. First I took off and ran into another classroom. Then when I realized I ought to escape before I am caught, I ran into the boiler room.

That did scare me a bit, but it wasn't the loud machines. It was Mr. Finnegan, the janitor. He was big and gruff looking. He had the most hairiest looking arms and face I ever did see. I'm not

sure what he said to me but it was loud anyway. I jumped up, spun around, and ran right out the door. Now I had poor Mummy chasing me around the outside of the building in the cold. She drove the pram with Dessie bouncing his chubby head up and down the whole way.

This went on for quite a while. Mummy shouting for me to come and me shouting, "No!" back at her.

Mum tells me she was completely mortified when Mrs. Lanigan came outside with a few teachers to give her a hand. One of them was a schoolmate of Mum's when she was my age. She still lives over the road from our house but is not a teacher now. Dad says it's because she knew I was coming there in the fall. Mum says he is ridiculous. Her friend was expecting a baby. Mum said she just wanted to stay home with her baby and that's all.

Even the principal couldn't make me budge that day outside the school. I was so proud to have them all eating out of my hands. Well, that was until Mummy decided to just pack up little Dessie and head home. She was leaving without me. At first I remember standing there wondering what I was going to do with myself.

And the rain was also helpful in my decision making process. I looked at Mummy, who was by now in the car and driving away for real. Then I looked at Mrs. Lanigan who had a very mean, stern look on her face.

But when Mr. Finnegan came out of the building I ran like a greyhound. I went down the hill, through the gate and into the car park. I ran as fast as my legs could take me.

I didn't want to miss my car ride. I say we are from Miltown Malbay to folks I meet but our farm is over a mile away from the school. And that is a mighty long walk in the rain. It is **REALLY** long when you have short legs like I did when I was almost 4.

It would be great if the story ended there. But I cannot disappoint you. I have to tell you what happened next.

You see, there was a big boulder just in front of the car park. And I didn't see it. It was staring me up in the face, too. I was too worried about Mummy leaving for home to notice it.

I should have paid attention, but back then I found it impossible.

That lovely boulder just boldly sat there waiting for my impulsive self to land on it.

And land on it I did. Smack down on top of the most pointiest part of it. I put a giant gash in my stubborn head. I needed ten stitches in my left eyebrow and that is only the outside ones.

This was me, seconds before impact....

My mother claims it was penance for my wicked behavior that day. She also maintains that she never took the car out of gear either. But if my memory serves me correctly, she was practically out of the car park when my head hit that pesky stone.

That day has forever been marked in my mind as the start of the problem for me. It is my earliest memory, to be honest.

Mum says that was nowhere near the real start of the problem. She says I was born with a short fuse and busy backside. What she means by that is that I was a very cranky baby who pooped a lot. I mean **A LOT**.

She said I topped both my brothers combined in poop production by the time I was three. Dad just looks at it from the money side. He says that when it comes to University, I'm going to get a few thousand Euros less money to make up for all the extra diaper expenses I cost them in my first three years of life.

Mum says not to mind him. As long as I keep reading all the time like I do, she will help me with University fees herself. She said if that means letting Dad fend for himself at dinnertime while she goes working, then so be it.

So now you know how my life as a known National School trouble maker really got started. It happened long before I ever set foot in the junior infants class that September. I was a marked man even when I was still in diapers and Mrs. Lanigan never **EVER** forgot that wild first impression I gave her.

Chapter 4

ACCIDENTS SEEMED TO HAPPEN, A LOT....

I didn't want to be a bad kid. I just couldn't help myself. Dad says that deep down he raised me to be a thoughtful boy and I've never let him down yet.

I really like my Dad. He is outside and around the farm almost the whole time though. So mostly Mum is the one dealing with me. She usually sticks me in the corner when I'm bad. She says that idle minds are the devil's playground. She likes to send me out to work with Dad as much as she can.

Dad says being outside clears his head. What he means by that is simple. When you are outside and on

This is Dad relaxing on the bonnet of his tractor. We call the 'hood' a 'bonnet' in Ireland. And we call the 'trunk' a 'boot'. Isn't that funny?

---

your own you get time to think a lot. He thinks about things while he works. He says it is a good way to keep yourself out of trouble, too. Mum always gets upset when I am bad but Dad is a soft touch. He almost never gets upset with me. He mostly just talks to me about things. Then he makes me go off and think a lot. I like to have quiet time for myself but I don't always think about the right things. That's the problem.

Dad said when I was a wee fella I told everyone in advance when I knew I was going to be naughty. When the feeling came over me I thought it was my duty to give everyone a fair warning. Dad says I'm the reason Mum has to buy hair dye now. Mum says that's ridiculous. She's not grey, she just isn't really blonde anymore without a little help from the hairdresser.

Nana used to tell Mum not to worry. She had six kids herself and they all turned out just fine. She was sure that I would eventually settle down in my own time.

Mum didn't feel the same way, though. She was afraid I would turn into a dosser.

She made it her business to over-correct me every chance she got. I think I made her feel like a failure as a mother with all my constant badness every day.

So to handle my daily tantrums Mum started using parenting help books to get me to behave better. She was sure a better, more professional technique like Dr. Phil's or the Super Nanny's would do the trick. We did naughty spots, quiet times, and something called planned ignoring. We did a few other ones I don't remember off the top of my head, too. I liked the charts

I did this in the sitting room. Mum was not happy.... Are you wondering what I mean when I say dosser? Well, in Ireland it means about the same thing as what my cousins in America call a bum. It's like a poor little waif. Now there's a word for you. Dessie wants me to tell you to look it up. Go ahead and do it. My story can wait. But hurry up!

and stickers, but mostly I just drove Mum crazy.

In the end nothing really helped me get happy with myself. I was still an ornery boy working on a career as a future dosser. Mum and Dad couldn't really do anything about that.

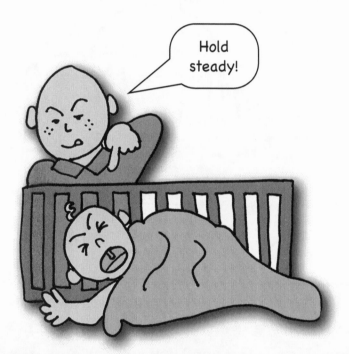

I didn't really want to include a picture of this. But Mum said it would serve as a good motivation to do the right thing the next time I got one of those urges.

This next part isn't exactly fun to talk about but I have to tell it like it is. It was pure tomfoolery. That's what Dad said when he came in the door that night.

I think what happened on this day was the clincher for Mum. It happened about two weeks after Ronan was born. I don't remember all the details exactly. I do recall getting paddled on my rear end for nearly killing him in his cot.

I almost smothered him with a huge pillow. I wasn't mad at anyone or anything.

But Mum wasn't sleeping much those days and was stretched pretty thin. According to Mum she must have told me a gazillion times to stop whatever it was that I was doing to him. She was in the back kitchen and I was happily trying to sneak a little torture treatment in while she wasn't looking.

I was sort of humming and making these funny beep noises and stuff. I really didn't hear her saying anything to me at all. I was just feeling a bit goofy. I can't explain it other than this weird urge to do something bad. I just had to irritate him a little bit. Something inside me was just driving me to do it. I decided it might be interesting to touch his eyeball with my finger while it was open. I wanted to see if he would close it before my finger made contact. I really didn't consider what I might do when he started crying uncontrollably because his eyeball was sore.

So I made a knee-jerk reaction. I grabbed the big sofa pillow and covered his mouth with it so Mum wouldn't hear him crying and blame me for it.

This turned out to be a very dumb idea.

Well, okay. That's all I'm going to say about that business. You don't need to know all the dirty details about my life. Some things are better left to the imagination. I will just tell you that I never tried to poke someone's eyes out ever again.

I was spiraling out of control pretty fast back then. Funny thing, I sort of knew it, too. I definitely didn't want to do bad stuff, either. I just couldn't stop myself from losing the plot. That's an Irish way of saying that I lost my temper a lot.

A week later I got caught at school for pushing a classmate while we were in the toilet. He didn't wash his hands and I told him to. When he didn't listen I gave him a right good shove into the urinal. He almost cracked his head. Well, Mum was not too happy. She had to drop everything for an emergency meeting at the school. I barely remember what happened. I just remember acting silly while they talked. My teacher told Mum that she had never seen a boy act so poorly before in her entire life.

Mum drove all the way home without saying a word. But when we got in the door she really laid into me for mortifying her so badly at the school. Do you know what that means? She gave me a real harsh talking to. That's what she did.

She said that Mrs. Lanigan had half a mind to kick me out of school completely. The next time I laid a hand on another student I would be out of junior infants for good. I asked Mum if that meant I could just stay home with her for the rest of my life.

She got a wicked look in her eyes and said, "No, Cilie!" in a sharp tone. "You are halfway through your grade already. If they kick you out you will have to repeat the whole year all over again in September."

Then Mum sat down in the chair with her cup of tea and started to cry. I felt like a right good heel when she did that.

Chapter 5

GOODIE: THE PORRIDGE OF PAIN....

When I was four and even long before that, food was always an issue for me. Mum was always goading and cajoling me to eat something.

Breakfast was probably the best and only meal of the day that I truly enjoyed. After that I would just pick at my lunches and dinners. Well, let me just tell you that I would often spend nearly all evening long at the dinner table. So much so that I carved grooves in the top of it with my spoon. Dad was less than thrilled with me for that.

Mum was cross too but managed to use that as an excuse to find a good placemat to leave down over my spot.

I often had to hold my grumbling belly for a long while after eating. I didn't like to eat much.

Mornings in our house are always hectic, even though there aren't any girls in our family except for Mum. I am always late. I am famous for forgetting stuff like my shoes and underwear, too.

By the time night comes I'm completely knackered and my brain only works at about fifty percent. That's why Mum always makes me do my homework right after school. Sometimes I even wait to do it until after breakfast if we are busy all afternoon, but Mum told me not to put that in my book so whatever you do, don't tell my teacher that!

Um, I meant to do that.

Once I was so tired at night that I even put my pajamas on over my clothes when I was getting ready for bed. Dad had a good laugh that night. He said I am an absent minded professor all right. I have my nose buried in my books the whole time. He says it gives me a half-cooked brain at bedtime. But he's only messing with me.

My favorite breakfast of all was always goodie back in the old days. It was the only thing Mum could be guaranteed I would eat before school. Most other stuff was just yucky to me. Granddad says that his mum made goodie for him when he was a boy, too. I liked the way that Nana used to make it for me the best. She put two slices of day old bread in a saucepan with TWO

spoons of sugar instead of one and a glass of Dad's creamy thick milk.

That is still the only way that Granddad will eat it, with fresh milk from the tank in Dad's shed. He says that the jugs in the store are pure poison and that they take all the good stuff out of it. Nana says he just likes to drink his milk for free rather than pay the store for it. Don't tell Nana, but I think I'm with Granddad on that one. Although, to be honest, it's been a while since I've had goodie. My memory isn't 100 percent on the taste anymore.

But back in the day I probably ate a bowl or two of goodie each morning for a year. I started when I was three. By the time I was 5 my goodie had started to go bad for me. Dad nicknamed it my porridge of pain because I always managed to get me a nice ripe tummy ache after eating it. Mum said it was probably all that sugar.

Every evening I would get wicked, especially with 3 year-old Dessie who was always getting into all my stuff. He especially liked my Peppa the Pig house and my toy Legos. Usually I would try to punch him and stuff. I did actually bite him once or twice too. Mum and Dad were forever trying to talk sense into me. I spent a lot of time in the corner but it never seemed to help my temper in the long run.

Mum didn't take any notice of my tummy aches for a while because I always managed to complain about them at the same time I was getting in trouble for something. But eventually I started having some strange things happening to me that really put Mum and Dad thinking.

Chapter 6

POOP TALK

The first thing that started happening to me was a reoccurring white frothy poop. It was really gross. Then I started pooping out pieces of my dinner, like a chunk of a carrot or a whole pea. Once I ate a bag of raisins and nuts. Wouldn't you know, I could have picked them out of my poop the next day. I could have then rinsed them off and put them back into the bag. No one would have known the difference.

I had a lot of evil

Doc Curtin went to medical school in London. That's in England. He moved back home to Ennistymon after he finished. He was Mum's doc when she was a girl.

---

feelings for Dessie in those days. He definitely would have been the one I would have served them to. But I know I'm a good Catholic, because Nana always tells me I am. And God would not take too kindly toward me if I did something like that to my brother.

So it was shortly after that when we first visited the doctor at the clinic. I think Mum was looking for some answers. She quite often referred to me as a real plonkster. I'm still not sure what that means but I know it's not good. I asked Dad one time and he said with a chuckle that plonksters were on a television program that was a bit before my time.

So Mum finally made an appointment for me and Ronan together. She kept me out of school that day to take me. So for that I was really, really happy. I didn't mind school as a whole when I was little. It's just that I found sitting in the chair and listening to my teacher all day long was more torture than Dessie could have ever prepared me for. I mean, what was the point of having all those lovely toys around if half the day no one was allowed to play with them?

But in the car on the way down I was nervous about visiting the doctor. I wasn't sure if I would be getting a shot or having blood taken out. I wasn't quite feeling like the tough little boy Granddad always says I am. I heard Dad talking with Mum the night before. He said he didn't have much faith in Doc Curtin. He told Mum that all she was going to get after the visit was an empty checkbook.

Well, Doc's office is all the way in Ennistymon, and for a 4-year-old that's a long, long, long drive. For an adult it's about half-an-hour. Mum was driving in the car and had me pretty well sandwiched in the back between Ronan and Dessie. Geeze, was I smooshed back there. And worse yet, she had me holding one of those gross rubber dodies in Ronan's mouth so he wouldn't cry.

That's when it hit me. I mean, really, really hit me. We were coming around the bend into downtown Lehinch when I felt the first rumble.

"Mum."

"What?"

"I need to use the toilet."

"What? Now? Can't you wait until we get there?"

"Um, uh...."

That is the exact moment it happened. I got a terrible rumble in my innards and this sort of weird flash of pain. I was pretty used to that sort of thing at this stage. It pretty much happened every time I took a poop.

But while I was sitting in the car that day I felt a strange hot burning feeling in my butt and a nasty pressure to ooze something liquidy out. I looked down at Ronan. Then I smelt it. It was a cross between a hard boiled egg and slurry. At first I thought it was just a wet fart. It was nasty smelling. Then a split second later I realized my bum felt wet and hot.

Then Mum looked back. She asked if everyone was okay. I just sat there, looking at Ronan. I wished I was the one wearing a diaper. Or better yet, I wished Ronan was the one with the oozy poop stuck to his butt.

Of course the doc was real concerned when Mum went and told him my embarrassing story. He said that wasn't normal and neither was my height and weight.

Doc Curtin thought I might just have a touch of a bug. He said I needed to eat more fats to put some meat on my bones. He thought some heavy cream, loads of yogurt, which I hated, and a bit of butter might do the trick. Mum agreed with him.

Back then everyone in my house knew I was the number one pickiest eater in the family. Back then trying to get me to eat new things was a full time job with no benefits. I was way more picky than Sean and trust me, that is saying something. He used to make his mum peel the skins off off his sausages before he would eat them. I was way worse. If it wasn't bread I pretty much didn't like it.

Mum told the doc that she was a bit worried that my problems were more serious than that. I just seemed to catch every bug floating around the school. And she was at her wits' end on how to deal with me when I got ornery, which was becoming a regularly scheduled event in our house.

So Mum went home and got busy including heavy cream and butter. She was also literally spoon feeding the yogurts into me any chance she could. Dad gave me a full glass of milk from the tank every night after he finished milking. The cream was so thick I could write my name in it. After a few weeks I came down with a serious case of croup. That landed me back in Doc Curtin's office with a double ear infection and a barking seal cough that made breathing tricky for me.

Mum said, "Well, I don't think the milk agrees with him. He's not ornery when he's sick, but the poor lad is so weak. There's got to be something we're missing."

Doc agreed and said he had a hunch there might be something wrong all right. He thought there was a problem with the way I was digesting my food. He said there was a disease called celiac sprue and he was pretty sure I had it. He wanted to run a test to be absolutely certain.

He rolled up my sleeves and took out a needle the size of a pencil with a huge fat barrel at the bottom of it.

"What's that?" I said.

"Just make a fist Cilie and close your eyes. "'Tis just a little pinch is all." Doc replied.

"He's just going to take a sample of your blood, love." Mum encouraged.

My eyes bulged. "Blood?!"

"Not to worry, old boy. I have a little coin that helps me do the trick."

"You have a trick?" I asked.

"Yes I do. You see, I put this little plastic coin with all these tiny bumps on it and I put it on your arm like this.

Does that hurt?"

"Well, no-" I said honestly.

"Then I put the needle in the hole at the center of the coin and take your blood out."

"NO!" I shouted, pulling my arm back.

"Just watch me Cilie."

"I can't!" I said.

You better believe I looked away. I may be tough but I'm definitely not soldier material.

"Cilie-- Are you ready?"

"No." I said, holding back tears.

"Well, it's too late. I'm done old boy!"

After that day I had a new found appreciation for old Doc Curtin. He was and still is number one in my book. Before we left he told Mum to give it a couple of weeks for the results.

That was the slowest 14 days of my mother's life, or so she says now. I think she is exaggerating. I was ten days overdue when she was pregnant with me and I think that it took her much, much more patience to wait for me to be born than it took for those couple of weeks.

As we were leaving his office, Doc said not to worry until the test comes back positive. But it seems like that was all Mum did for those two straight weeks.

She worried non-stop. I think it drove myself and Dad up the walls.

Mom knew that Doc was pretty certain this was going to be my problem. He told her it is quite common in Ireland and they actually call it an Irish disease as a joke. There are many Irish people with it. He said that Galway, which is just over the border from where I live in Clare, at one time reported the highest number of celiacs per population in the whole wide world. But that was a long time ago.

This made me wonder about other kids like me. Exactly how many were there with oozy poop problems and sore tummies?

"So how many Irish kids have it?"

"Well, Cilie, how many boys and girls are at your school?"

"I'm not sure."

"How many are in your class?"

"20."

"And your school has about 8 classes, so that means there are about 160 boys and girls at your school."

He paused a second and leaned down.

"So statistically speaking, Cilie, there might be one boy or girl at your school with celiac sprue."

"Well, what if I'm that boy?" I asked.

"We'll see about that." He answered.

Then Mum and Doc started talking more technical and they sort of lost me. I hadn't a clue what they were going on about so I asked why Doc thought we needed a special store for me.

"Not to worry, Cilie, old boy. We won't make any plans for special stores until after the results come back. You just hang in there. But do stay away from the goodie and the milk until I see you again in two weeks, just in case."

Chapter 7

UNDER ATTACK

Stay away from the goodie?

You know what I did all the way home in the car after hearing that prescription. And Doc told me that just when I was deciding that I liked him....

Okay, I won't undignify myself by telling you in writing exactly what happened after we left his office. Just look at the picture on the next page. Judge for yourself what happened for a whole half-an-hour all the way home from Ennistymon in the car with Mum.

At home Dad was ever so optimistic, as usual. He thought for sure I didn't have that thing called celiac. Mum, on the other hand was totally convinced that I did.

Did you notice that the steering wheel is on the right side of the car in Ireland? We drive on the left side of the road too. That sure is confusing to Americans who visit!

She was ready to clean out the presses in the back kitchen that night. Dad just put on the kettle and plopped down at the table with a big knife and a loaf of fresh white bread from the bakery. He shaved off a piece about an inch thick and then loaded it with some butter and a spoonful of sugar on top.

I love Dad, I really do, but I have to say that on that particular night he was torturing me worse than anything I'd ever done to Dessie or Ronan. All he needed to do to turn that concoction into goodie was throw it in the saucepan and pour a cup of milk all over it.

Mum just put this look on her face as she watched Dad cut a second slice.

"That stuff is pure poison, you know. I'm convinced."

"Well I feel perfectly fine. All these years and I'm not dead yet."

"You know, Doc says it's hereditary. If Cilie has it then one of us probably has it too."

Dad just let out a funny chortle, "S'pose I've got to die of something anyway."

I wanted to plop down next to Dad and steal a slice but Mum was watching so I just tiptoed out of the back kitchen and down to the room I shared with Dessie.

He was coloring on the walls again. Normally I would have tried to bully the crayons off of him. I was really tired after the visit to Doc's office, though. I didn't feel much like it. And to be honest, I was so hungry I could eat a scabby donkey.

"Can I have a turn?" I asked.

"In a minute."

"C'mon. Just give me the darn crayon."

"NO. I have to finish this one piece."

"What are you drawing?"

"A pig."

"Peppa the Pig?"

"Yes."

"Well you're not doing it right. You have to make the nose bigger and the eyes smaller."

Dessie just looked at me in utter amazement. I think he was shocked that I wasn't grabbing the crayon out of his hands or anything.

"Never mind. Hey, why do you do that all the time?"

"Cause you never let me have any paper," he answered.

"You blame me for everything," I said.

But, you know what? Back then he was probably right. I was like that to him a lot.

After that I just left him to his artwork and climbed into my bed to read a book. I didn't feel much like talking anymore anyway. It had been a long day and I had a lot to think about.

Dessie was only 3 that night. Now he's seven, and he's asking me to tell you that he doesn't color on the walls in our room anymore. I have to write this or he told me he will steal my computer and erase that whole part out of this story.

Brothers.

Such pains in the neck.

So this is my official clarification everybody. Dessie, I hope you are happy now. And if you are reading this part I hope you start to just MIND YOUR OWN BUSINESS and stop READING my stuff!

Oh, and Dessie, you should have seriously considered my artistic advice. I do take after Mum, you know. Maybe next time....

Oh, and by the way Dessie, **NO** you cannot erase this because I put in a password!

Ha, ha, Dessie.

Oh, and for the record everybody, this here is the dumb pig Dessie drew on the wall. It doesn't even have a body and he didn't even stay in the lines.

Now here is a pig that I drew. Honestly now, why wouldn't Dessie just admit that I am the pig master?

Now where was I? Oh yes, I was talking about not eating goodie and possibly being a celiac.

I spent two whole weeks without goodie while we waited. I figured after two weeks Doc would tell me that I checked out fine and could go right home and have another bowl of the good stuff. After all, the croup was gone, the pain in my ear was gone, and I had to admit, my tummy was feeling a small bit better.

Well, the next time we saw Doc Curtin he was armed with a boat load of information. Apparently Mum's hunch was right. Doc explained to us that the goodie was actually making me sick. I had to stop eating gluten or else I would get very, very ill. He said I would get more sick than just the bad case of croup like I had a few weeks back. He said the gluten protein in the wheat makes my body attack itself. Doc explained that I could get all kinds of new problems if I kept eating that way. Stuff like my kidneys, skin, intestines, and glands could get affected. Actually, he said that the gluten was already starting to do that stuff to me, but I just wasn't a bad case yet.

He asked if I had any questions.

"Can I eat cake?"

"No."

"Can I eat bread?"

"No."

"How about a chicken burger?"

"No, Cilie. I'm really sorry but all those things are off the list."

"Hm. What's on the list?"

"All sorts of good foods like apples and bananas, and carrots, and potatoes, and rice."

"Well, I don't like that list."

Mum shot me a sad, knowing look. I think she understood.

Then they started talking to each other about all kinds of stuff that was not interesting to me anymore. Mum had lots of questions. I just wound my fingers around the blood pressure cord tied to the wall. It hadn't really sunk in yet, to be honest.

I had heard all I wanted to hear about this problem. I had to figure out a way to eat cake again once and for all. Some how, some way, I was going to do it. My whole happiness in the entire world depended on it.

Chapter 8

MY OFFICIAL CELIAC REPORT

Well, I figure I should add my Celiac report from 2nd class about now. This seems like a really good spot to plonk it down. I actually wrote it two years after Doc gave me the bad news but trust me, if I had written it when I was 6 you'd be looking at a bunch of scribbly letters and eraser marks. I was still pretty bad student in 1st class. Most of my papers had a red "Sloppy" written all over them. Dad says it's a good thing I like to read a lot. But the best libraries aren't in West Clare. So when my 2nd class teacher gave us science reports to do I asked to go to Ennis. Dad promised to take me one Saturday after the mart.

These are the raised bogs in Clare. Bogs are areas of peat that get a lot of rain. Peat are decaying plants and trees. Once a year we go in and cut the bogs and stack them like this until they dry. Then we take the "turf" home and burn it in our stoves.

We loaded up the trailer and then I got to sit in the front seat of the car all the way down. We didn't chat much because the news was on Clare FM and Dad always listens to it for the full half hour. We passed the bogs and went through Connolly. I like that road because my ears always pop on the way back down into Ennis. Mum hates it because she says it is a dangerous road through the mountains. So Dad and I only go that way when we are alone together in the car. It is a pretty narrow road that winds around the mountain.

Dad just winked at me when he passed the Ennis Road and said, "We're a couple of cheeky school boys, eh?" I smiled at him. I knew exactly what he meant. We were a couple of bold and daring boys, all right.

After the mart Dad stayed outside with the trailer full of cows to wait for me. He said, "So it's time to go see a man about a dog, eh?" I said, "Na, the librarian is a woman." He just chuckled. He was only having me on. Granddad has said that about a million times himself. That is an old saying.

The lady behind the desk was nice when I met her. I told her all about my project idea for school. She said it was an impressive undertaking for such a small boy. I just smiled.

I used to get that a lot more when I was 4 and even a bit when I was 5, but after that I really started to grow again. This year I'm actually not much shorter than my classmates. And now people don't ever confuse me for Dessie anymore.

That is a HUGE relief. I can't even tell you.

Dad used to always say he would get me a T-shirt that read: "I'm the big brother," if only times weren't so

70

tough. I never found that funny. Shortness is not something to joke about, especially when it is YOU who is SHORT.

Mum used to tell me not to mind him that he was only blaggarding me. Now he's got nothing to say because I've grown four whole inches and am way taller than Dessie.

Anyway, back to my library story. The nice librarian probably thought I was a really smart 6 year old and not anywhere near 2nd class or something. People used to think my brother Dessie was my twin. Ha! Now I'm so much taller that I can give him a deadner. Do you know what that is? It is when you hit someone's thigh with your knee. You know, you give a lad a knee in his thigh. It is something the lads on the football field do when they are messing around with their teammates.

Once I said I was going to do that to my American cousin and I swear he just looked at me like I was speaking Chinese or something. Dessie hates when I do that but it's long overdue payback. Plus it keeps him out of my stuff most times.

I remember that the librarian that day told me I ought to get my Mum to join the Celiac Society of Ireland. She even wrote it down on a piece of paper so I wouldn't forget. Then she even printed some stuff out from her computer to help me with my report.

It took a few days to write the report. Mum helped me a bit with wording it, but I am proud to say that the drawing and the caption were totally my own stuff. I didn't get any help with that part. My teacher was fierce impressed with my efforts and I scored a 10 out of 10. I was so delighted with myself. Dad and Mum even saved the report in a nice plastic folder for me to admire.

I made a copy of it for you to look at. So anyway, here it is, but listen, I'm trusting you not to copy it for your own science report at school. That is called cheating and it is against the rules.

Don't do it....

Or else....

I'll tell your teacher!!!!

"All About Celiac Disease"
By Cilie Yack

One in every 133 people in the world have Celiac disease. If you have it you cannot eat gluten which is the protein found in wheat, barley, rye and oats.

When you have celiac your body makes these little antibody soldiers called gliadins so that they can go after the gluten that you eat and kill them. But the problem is, your body goes and makes two different troops with two different commanders. The one troop goes in to kill the gluten but the other troop, called the T-cells, accidentally goes in and kills the villi guys living in the small intestine.

That is a big problem because your body needs the villi to smoosh up your foods and feed them to the rest of your body. Without the villi men you start to starve even though you are eating your goodie, bread, and your sticky buns every day. So basically your army is all confused and stuff.

Then the body doesn't get fed right and you get sick. The only way to cure this problem and stop the war is to stop eating the gluten. If the enemy gluten soldiers don't invade the small intestine then the gliadin soldiers put down their weapons and make a treaty with the villi men .

After a while the villi men start working again but they are so badly injured from the war that it takes them a while to get strong enough to do their jobs.

Finally everything gets better. The celiac starts to digest food again like a normal person. And that is what it is like to have celiac disease.

Drawing and Caption by Cilie Yack

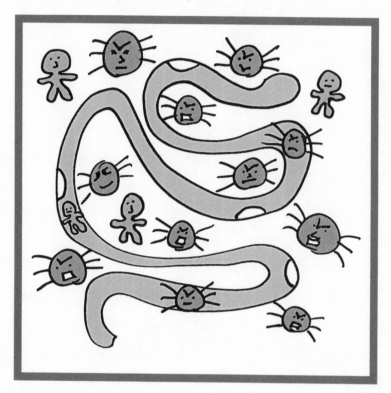

The long pink hose is the small intestine. The gingerbread men are the glutens. The six-legged men are the gliadins. The troops with their mouths open are attacking the glutens. The ones with their mouths closed are attacking the villi. The circles are broken bits from the villi men who don't have any weapons and are getting killed the whole time by their own men.

Chapter 9

SNEAKY AND CHEEKY....

Well I'm over the moon, absolutely flabbergasted. You will never guess who just called Mum and offered to give ME a tour of the behind the scenes action at Dromoland Castle Hotel. Guess, Guess, GUESS!

Okay, have you figured it out yet? Oh, never mind. You will never in a million years figure it out. You probably won't even believe me when I tell you. It is so amazing it's crazy.

The executive chef called, that's who! He is so amazingly famous. He has cooked for two American Presidents already in his life *AND* he is younger than Dad. He even lived in Dublin and in London for a while.

Now he has the top job at Dromoland which is right here in Ennis.

Ha! You are probably thinking, "Why in the world would a famous chef be calling a future dosser?" Because, I am telling you one thing for certain. I am NO future dosser. I can't wait to go. I am going to ask Mum if it would be okay for me to bring my cousin Sean and my best friend Dermot.

Oh, yes, that's right. I haven't told you about Dermot have I? I'm so sorry about that. I'm afraid I've jumped ahead of myself again. It is just that I got so excited about the call. I forgot where I was in the story. Now I realize I haven't even told you about Dermot (actually, I call him Derm most times). He is my closest friend in the whole world.

Derm lives over the road from us, down by the cross to be exact. That's just a country way of saying he lives on the intersection at the end of our road. I am at his house nearly every day and we play football on the same team, St. Joseph's GAA. It is our second year in football and we play for the same club that our dads played for when they were boys. Derm is one of the finest players on our team. He scores a lot of goals. Everybody likes him both on the field and off. I'm a cornerback which means I block and defend the goals. I'm really aggressive on the field, but I don't have the style that Derm has. He can carry the ball from one end of the field to the other with precision. Do you know what that means? Our manager says when you have precision you are very skilled with the ball.

I know the three things that can make you a great footballer:

1. *You need to be a good dribbler.*

2. *You have to be able to pass at times.*

Here is a picture of Derm with his foot on the ball. Gaelic football is a little bit like soccer and a little like rugby. We kick the ball into the goal and over it. Of course goals are worth 3 points and kicking it over is only worth one point. So you have to add and multiply if you want to keep score!

3. You don't want to lose the ball so don't kick it too hard.

We learn a lot of stuff like that when we go to training. I usually get a lift from Dad, my uncle, or Derm's dad. The three of us lads always ride together. Derm is great when it comes to being a friend. Once I figured that out we've been best friends.

Derm and I go way back-- all the way to junior infants class when we were 4. And I probably never said it, but he was the boy I shoved into the urinal the day Mrs. Lanigan almost kicked me out of school.

And of course he never forgot that.

And neither did I.

Or my mum.

Well we didn't get on great in the beginning as you can tell. When he turned 6 his mum invited me to his birthday party. She let me come even though I clobbered him in the toilets.

My mum said that I could go but I better act like a gentleman or she would plunk my rear end in the corner until I turned fifteen.

Naturally I intended on being a perfect angel after that. The problem is, well, I just wasn't quite yet out of my impulsive stage yet.

I still had a lot to learn.

Let me explain....

Mum dropped me off with my own lunch box that evening. She figured I was all sorted out for the party. I

think she was planning on going to the hairdressers or something.

I was delighted. I couldn't wait to be on my own without my mum for a change.

I was carrying a small wrapped box for Derm with a card I made. I was pretty impressed with myself. I had bought him a present that I really wanted. How many

81

people do you know that actually do **THAT**? It was my way of making it up to him. You know, for pushing him in the toilets.

The first thing I eyed was the snack table. As a matter of fact, I was very obsessed by it. I couldn't help myself. Mum had been so crazy about food that she made me think about it all the time. And it wasn't in a good way either. All I did was think about what I was missing. It never crossed my mind to think about what I *COULD* have.

That was my whole problem back then. When everyone around you is munching on chips and finger sandwiches you start to feel sorry for yourself. It is only natural to be jealous of them.

I remembered worrying about my Spiderman lunchbox. I didn't want to open it and look like a real traveling freak show. Being different is an invitation to "call notice to yourself." That is an Irish way of saying that you make everyone notice you. Some kids like that. They might want to be a famous television comedian like Brendan Grace or something when they grow up. They probably have a lot of confidence in themselves.

When I was six I wasn't like that at all. I did not want other kids to notice me like that. Back then I had a bad case of wanting to be normal. Now I don't care so

much. I know it is because I found out what I am good at. Now the other kids admire me a little bit.

Oh, and did I mention that on that night I was a whole six months without one bowl of goodie, a single biscuit, a slice of cake or anything?

I was so ready to have one night to feel totally normal. For the first time Mum wasn't watching over me with a raised eyebrow. And believe me Derm's party was the perfect night as far as I was concerned.

Let me tell you, Mum dropping me off into that place and driving away was the craziest thing she could have done. I guess she figured she could trust me.

Well, she figured wrong.

The temptation was too great.

Derm's mum knew I couldn't eat the cake or the egg sandwiches. But I knew there was no way possible she could keep her eyes on me the whole time. Now I certainly didn't mind skipping those smelly egg sandwiches she made. I absolutely hate egg salad; but I was drooling over that chocolate cake she had picked up from the bakery in town.

(Meet Mr. Egg Salad. I call him Eggie.)

How come no one wants to play with me? What, do I smell or something?

When it was time for Derm to open the presents I asked to use the toilet. Instead of going there I snuck into the back kitchen and grabbed a chunk of that half-eaten chocolate cake.

This is just an unflattering look at me stuffing my face with chocolate cake at Derm's house. Most Irish families have little fridges like this one in their kitchens.

I wish I could tell you that it wasn't good or something. I am not going to lie. It was really delicious. I found myself shaving the bits stuck to the bottom of the box with my fingernails and licking them to get every last crumb.

I must have been gone a while when the door pressed open. It was Derm. He saw both me and the cake but he said nothing. I knew right then and there that he was a true friend. I decided I liked him for real at that very moment.

I only lived up the road from Derm. When the party ended his mum asked him to walk me halfway back and then come home. She knew my mum was still getting her hair done and my dad was home alone with the young lads.

Derm and I only got a few feet from the cross when I started to feel strange. I got the urge to swallow some sort of lump in my throat. We kept walking a bit but the funny feeling never settled down. I was starting to get a bit worried. I didn't remember Doc Curtin ever saying what might happen if I cheated on my diet. I know what you are thinking. How come this didn't matter to me while I was cleaning the cake plate? Well, I just never thought about anything but cake. But on the way home I was really getting concerned.

Halfway there I had to stop. I just bent over because I was getting sort of nauseated. I found that I needed to swallow a lot because my mouth was really getting wet with spit.

Then it happened. My guts started heaving and spewing. I literally puked my guts out all over the side of the road. Chocolate cake littered the roadside as if it had never been digested at all. I was mortified. Derm was standing beside me the whole time watching me get sick.

Then he asked if I was okay after I finished the last puke. I shook my head "yes" in a hesitant way. He sort of chuckled.

"What's so funny?" I asked, annoyed he was taking pleasure in my pain.

"Just thought I ought to clobber you for not washing your hands afterward."

I had to laugh out loud. Now that was funny!

"Are you sick?" he asked me.

"Naw. I think I am just having a reaction to that cake I ate."

"Well then you better keep off the stuff," he said. "It doesn't agree with you."

"I know. But I love cake. I'm going to have to learn how to make cake that tastes as good as that."

Derm smiled, "and then I can help you eat it."

"Yes, but don't puke it up afterwards!" I joked, even though I still felt pretty lousy.

We laughed together as we walked.

Right then and there I knew Derm and I would be friends for life.

Then he cracked a hilarious joke about Dad's cows licking my puked up cake off the road in the morning.

"Sick!" I said.

Derm laughed at me. Then we both chuckled a whole lot together before he had to make his way back home.

Hey, I thought that was milk.... No, wait....I think it's chocolate milk!

It gets pretty dark at night in the country. You wouldn't want to be caught on the roads or in the fields without a torch (that's a flashlight) after dusk. So I tried to hurry as fast as I could back to the house.

Well then, wouldn't you know Mum figured out what happened at Derm's house later on that night. She saw me puke one last time just when she walked in the door. Talk about having bad timing....

Dad was disappointed when he heard about what I had done at Derm's. But he completely understood. He said, "Well, Cilie, I suppose you don't miss the water until the well runs dry." And that about summed it up, really.

Believe me, and I swear it is true, I never, ever, EVER did something stupid like that again. I suppose I just needed to try it out just once to see if I am truly allergic or not.

Now I know I am.

Oh, and by the way-- I can guarantee that that Derm would never let me eat gluten again, either. My chocolate puke really grossed him out. He jokes with me all the time about it. We call it the "C.P." Those are the initials for "Chocolate Puke." It is sort of our secret code. Sometimes a kid will offer me a cookie or something. They will say, "Hey, do you want one?"

And then Derm will usually say, "Hey, do you want a C.P., Cilie?"

Then we just laugh because no one else knows what we are talking about.

He is sound down to the ground. That's what you say when you've got a really, really, REALLY great friend you can count on 100 percent. He totally and completely hates to see good food go to waste, too. Whenever we go to parties together he eats two pieces of bakery cake and I eat....

Oops!

I almost gave it away....

Chapter 10

KITCHEN CAPERS

First thing Monday morning Mum and I were back at Doc Curtin's for a visit. Mum was very upset after the party. She was also quite worried about my health, as usual. No matter how much I tried, I couldn't convince her that I was fine. After I puked Saturday night on the road with Derm I actually felt totally relieved.

"Cilie, you can't just keep eating gluten and puking it up."

"I know."

"Cilie, it doesn't work that way," she said as we waited for the doctor to come into our exam room.

Now that I'm a bit older I know why she was worried. But back then I was still just a little kid. That night I didn't know anything about gliadins or villi. I just knew that I wanted that cake.

I puked because my body somehow knew that had to get rid of the cake. If it didn't puke it out, then my little villi guys were going to get killed down there again. And after six months they were just starting to perk up and do their jobs. Just one night of cake could have really hurt them. But back then I didn't understand any of that stuff.

Doc padded the exam table and I gladly hopped up.

"How are we doing Cilie?"

"Great."

"Your Mum says you got caught in the long grass with a piece of chocolate cake."

"I did."

"Was it a good cake old boy?"

"Yes, it was absolutely the best most lovely chocolate cake ever. Derm's Mum got it from O'Connor's Bakery." Doc and Mum nodded in unison. Then things took a serious turn right there in the office.

And you know that they were going to....

"Don't get caught in the long grass" is an old Irish saying. Long grass is hard to walk in and can have bad things hiding in it. A kid could step into something dangerous. Doc was telling me to to be careful in a round about way.

Doc Curtin knelt down and looked me square in the eyes. He wasn't mad or anything but he definitely looked like he meant business.

"This is some serious stuff, Cilie."

Mum nodded in agreement again but she was surprisingly quiet.

"You can't go eating cake whenever you feel like it just because your Mum and Dad aren't watching."

"I know, but I love cake, and biscuits, and chicken burgers and goodie."

"But you don't want to feel sick," Mum added.

"Oh no. Definitely not."

Doc paused a second, then he straightened up and glanced at Mum.

"Mrs. Yack, why don't you and Cilie try your hand at a few gluten-free recipes?" Doc asked. "I think he might really like the challenge in the kitchen and he's a smart lad," he added.

Doc winked at me and smiled.

"Oh, yes, Mum, PLEASE!" I begged. I knew exactly what I wanted.

"Just remember, Mrs. Yack, that the kitchen has to be very clean," he warned. "You can't have any wheat flour hanging around the place, just in case," He said.

We left Doc's office and headed into the town centre to find the health food store that has all those alternative flours. We also got a nice helpful book that was going to get our back kitchen ready for the super challenge of teaching me how to cook.

The nice lady at the store told me she was celiac too. That was the first real person I had ever met with the same thing as me. All of a sudden I felt like I could really do this. She kept all kinds of neat snacks and foods in her store just for celiacs like us.

"You know, Cilie, we might be celiacs but we still have to eat!" She said with a wink. She even let me try a chocolate bar as long as Mum said it was okay. I was in chocolate heaven.

We bagged up our stuff and said thanks and goodbye. I couldn't wait to get started with my new foods.

Mum and I landed home with rice flour, tapioca flour, and potato flour. Then I had to tog out for my game. I was so excited that I ran all the way down to Derm's house in my gear. I couldn't wait to ask him if he wanted to come back with me to my house later. I couldn't wait to experiment with him.

That afternoon, we played against the lads in nearby Quilty. They are our rivals. We won because we scored 3 goals and 2 points while they only scored 2 points.

Ha! Ha!
**Quilty!
Better
Luck Next
Time!**

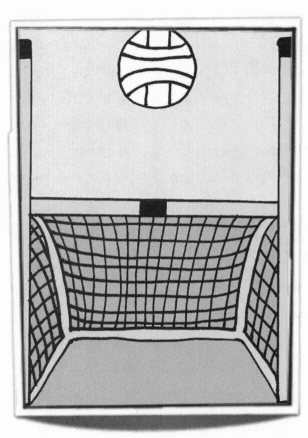

This is what the goal looks like in Gaelic Football. It's different from a soccer goal because we have two posts that go up the sides. This ball is going between the posts. That means the team that kicked it is getting 1 point. If it went into the net it would be 3 points.

Okay, now let's get back to the story....

Derm and I went into the kitchen and took out a big glass bowl. We poured a tea cup full of tapioca flour into it. Then we added a tea cup of water. We stirred it up really well with a kitchen fork. Then we put it in the microwave for two whole minutes.

We took it out with oven mitts because it was really, really hot. Then we let it sit for a while.

Do you know what we discovered? We had made a sticky play goo.

"Look, Derm--- BOOGERS!" I shouted.

"Hey, I can roll this up and stick it to the window and it's a bug trap!" he said.

"I can roll this into a ball and it will stay on my fingers." I answered.

"So?" he challenged.

"So then I can stick it to your back. Now you have a booger on your back!" I shouted as I slapped a big one up there.

Next thing I knew we had boogers flying everywhere. They landed on my face, my sleeves, the windows, the presses, the floor.

"And I can...." Derm shouted after I pelted him with a big one on his chest.

"Boys!" Mum shouted from the sitting room next door. "What are you doing in the kitchen?"

Well, that was a dose of reality calling. I looked around us. We had made a HUGE mess.

"Um, we're cooking, Mum," I answered.

Well my hesitation certainly got Mum on her feet fast. Let's just say she wasn't too happy to see fake boogers stuck all over the window. I won't go into too many details about how Derm and I had to clean it up. We did stand on the countertop and scrub that window glass until it sparkled. But we had fun anyway, peeling boogers off it and washing them down the drain, one by one.

Mum wants me to tell you not to try this at home. So don't try it at home. But if your mum let's you make it anyway I want to tell you one thing. When they are wetter they're even better! They go from sticky to slimy. So run them under a little cold water and you will have even more disgusting things to do with them. Oh, and don't mess up your mum's kitchen. Mums definitely do **NOT** like that!

When we were finished tidying up our mess Mum called us over to the computer. She showed us the Celiac Society of Ireland's website and forum.

We call our cabinets presses. We have them in our kitchens and our bedrooms. We also have a hot press. This is a big closet where we keep the hot water tank. We put shelves around it. We keep our towels and our sheets in there so they are always warm and dry.

She said that she posted a question about how to bake with gluten-free flours and someone in Dublin had already answered her.

In Ireland celiac is spelled coeliac. Did you know that there are celiac societies all around the world? They are great places to learn about safe foods and restaurants. Sometimes they have events too.

Derm and I were excited.

"What do you want to make, Cilie?" she asked me.

"How about jam drop cookies?" I answered. I wanted to try something pretty easy for our first recipe. "Derm has them at his house and he loves them."

"Okay! Let's figure out what we need!" Mum answered.

We made our list from the recipe that a celiac man in Dublin had posted. Then Mum piled us lads into the car and we drove down to the store for our ingredients.

Chapter 11

LEARNING THE ROPES....

I have to stop here for a minute just to tell you a few things. That first recipe was a long time ago. And I have to say, quite honestly, it didn't turn out so good. But it wasn't **THAT** bad either. There are lots of things to consider when you are baking, the first of which is how to measure right.

Believe me--- and trust me about one thing. When a kid goes without a cookie for over six months that first taste is a lot better than you think. Even if it kind of crumbles and falls apart a little bit when you bite into it, the cookie is still good. Derm said that his cookies at home were still better. I told him not to worry, by the end

Well, Dad tried to be helpful and encouraging. But sometimes it wasn't very helpful or encouraging....

of the year mine would be better than his. And you know what?

They *were*.

In the beginning EVEN the DOG wouldn't eat some of the mistakes I made. And trust me, that is saying something. My dog once ate Mum's watercolor paints and made bright blue and green poops afterward.

I'm a bit competitive that way. You just can't be a jibber. If you are afraid to try new things then you'll never find out what you are good at, now will you?

Cooking is like art. Do you like to draw a lot? Do you have fun with coloring? If you answered yes, you will absolutely love becoming a chef. Anybody can do it with a little effort and enough confidence. The most fun and colorful foods to work with are fruits and vegetables. They are my favorites.

Getting started isn't easy, though. You have to really want to do it. You also have to expect to make a few bad tasting things along the way.

But eventually, you will make a brilliant recipe. It might really get noticed by folks that you'd never imagine *might* take notice.

There are three things that I have learned since that first jam drop that are really, really important in the kitchen. Do you want to hear what they are?

Okay, here goes...

1. You really have to know how to measure stuff.

2. You have to read a lot of recipes.

3. You have to have an imagination and be willing to make a few mistakes before you get your masterpiece.

So that's pretty much what happened with me. I spent about a year experimenting in the kitchen with

Mum and Nana (but mostly Mum). Pretty soon we had our regular list of recipes for breads, cookies, and buns.

I still didn't have a cake that tasted as moist and soft as Derm's birthday cake from O'Connor's Bakery. But I wasn't going to give up just yet.

But, you know, being a chef is a lot more than being able to make a few sweets every now and then. Most of my favorite recipes are regular lunches and dinners. Lunch can be tricky when you have celiac, but it can also be really fun to make up. After a while I developed a real reputation at my school during lunch hour.

The lads were always and forever looking in my box to see what kind of crazy concoction I had come up with that day. I have been known to roll a slice of bacon with cream cheese with a pickle tucked in the middle. But that's not even unique enough for me anymore. Now I take it up another notch. I love to keep everyone guessing. Sometimes I quiz everyone to see if they can guess what's in it.

Dinner is even more fun.

And speaking of dinner, I learned that I could make my brothers eat things that they normally wouldn't touch. I just use a little devious manipulation and some help from my friend Derm. I'll give you an example.

Guacarollies are my favorite lunch snack. Everyone was talking about them and copying me for weeks after I made it up. Dessie still asks Mum to put them in his lunch, too.

Some days Derm stays for dinner. On this particular night Mum made broccoli and asparagus. It quite honestly smelled up the kitchen. Derm and I were in the sitting room playing cards. We joked about how it smelled as good as his mum's egg salad sandwiches.

Derm whispered to me, "It's pure stink, boy!"

I chuckled.

"Like fresh slurry," he added.

You do remember what slurry is, right? Well, in case you forgot I will remind you again. It's cow poop. My dad sprays it on the fields once a year to fertilize the grass and every time he does Mum has to lock up all the windows. She prays for a lashing of rain from heaven to get rid of the stink. Sometimes it lasts a whole week.

Now in all fairness, there is NO comparison between broccoli and slurry. Broccoli smells like fresh cut flowers in comparison. Derm was only having a laugh.

Okay, now back to my story about the stinky broccoli. Derm and I concocted a brilliant plan when we noticed Dessie and Ronan complaining that they wouldn't eat their dinners. Mum called us to the table. We innocently took our seats. Then we started begging Mum for extra veggies. She shot me a strange glance.

Dad knew we were up to something. I saw him lift one eyebrow in my direction.

Dessie wanted to know why we wanted more.

"Because they are so lovely and tasty," Derm said, practically kissing his broccoli as he ate it.

"No they're not," challenged Dessie.

"Yes they are," said Derm.

"Then I want some," said Dessie.

I knew he would take the bait.

"Me too!" shouted Ronan, who was now 3 years old and a pain in my pajamas.

"Well," Derm said in a long, slow drawn-out way, "There's only ONE big piece and ONE small piece, so we will have to have a competition for the big piece."

I tried so hard not to laugh. I had two cards in my pocket. We had already planned the whole thing out in the sitting room earlier.

"Hey, Cilie-- got any cards?"

"Actually, I do. I've got a jack and a king."

"Okay," Derm continued, "I'll put the two cards face down on the table like so. Now whoever gets the jack gets the big piece. Whoever gets the king gets the small piece. We'll let ol' Ronan go first. Which one do you want?"

"I want the jack," he said.

Derm and I busted our guts laughing. Even Dad cracked a smile. Then Ronan got mad. He didn't like being laughed at, so we quickly settled down. We didn't want to ruin the whole plan.

"Now, okay- Ronan, listen, you have to pick the card first, then you will find out if you got the jack or king."

The lads drew their cards and Ronan won the big piece. This started a fight with Dessie that caused Mum to dash out of the back kitchen with a knife still in her hand. Dad finally cut the two pieces down the center so each could have an equal amount.

Dad grinned at Derm and said he had natural talent as a future salesman. He also said he mightn't buy ocean view property in Tipperary from from him either. (In case you are wondering, Tipperary is in the middle of Ireland. It is awful far from the coast no matter which way you turn.)

Dad fancies himself a real comedian at times. By the way, not even one ounce of broccoli went to the dog that night. Which was probably all right by him.

Well I do apologize wholly and completely, now. I think I went off on a bit of a tangent there. I didn't mean to go off the subject of being a chef too much but I wanted to make a very important point that Niall Lynch taught me. He says that presentation and attitude are everything in the food world.

It's true.

Just consider what Derm and I did that night. We proved that we could get a 5-year-old and a 3-year-old to fight over eating plain broccoli boiled in salty water. How did we do it? We just adopted the right attitude.

Eventually I realized that I could show anyone how yummy and fun gluten-free food can be. I did it by just by having a good attitude. It took me a while to figure all that out. But boy, when I did a world of opportunity opened up for me. I've got to tell you, if you want to eat good tasting food then you've really got to CARE about it. You've got to love food, all kinds of food. I know I

Now Mum wants Derm to come for dinner when she makes brussels sprouts.

joked about the stinking broccoli. But when it is cooked right and it's included in the right kind of dish it can be very good. If you also add a special signature sauce on the side, then you have culinary heaven. This is what Niall Lynch says.

Like I told you before, cooking is an art. And Mum will tell you that a good artist will paint or draw a little EVERY day. She also says that a good artist isn't afraid to try something new.

So now the question you need to ask yourself is, "Am I an artist?" If the answer is yes, then read on to the next chapter. Find out once and for all how I went from Cilie Yack with celiac to chef Cilie Yack, **head chef** of my very own sous club for kids!

Chapter 12

I'LL HAVE CAKE, CAKE, AND MORE CAKE PLEASE....

So last October our Football Coach told us that the league was going to hold a bake sale in town. He said we need to raise money for field improvements. The league has been saving for field lights over the last couple years. Everybody was getting involved, from the over 21 players all the way down to the under 8s. Derm, Sean, and I are all under 10s. That just means we are under age 10. My team is made up of a solid bunch of lads. We really help each other out on the field and off. The lads are not bad in the kitchen, but in all honesty,

Mum loved it. Ronan loved it. I was proud. Dessie- He ate three pieces. And Dad made me promise to save one slice for his lunch. I finally had the perfect recipe....

none are as good as me. I have been experimenting in the kitchen for over two years now.

Take my cousin Sean, for instance. God bless him, but whatever you do, don't leave him in the kitchen unattended for too long. He's a fierce good footballer, but he's not in the kitchen much. You'll NEVER know what you're going to get from him when he does go in there, either. Once when I was over there he gave me an ice pop that he had made from one of those plastic mold sets.

It sounds normal anyway, doesn't it? I mean, how can a kid mess that up? You just take some juice, pour it in, put the lid on and freeze. Simple.

Okay, obviously you don't know my cousin. If you did you would realize that he always has to take it up a notch.

He's crazy I tell you.

I mean that in a good way.

So he gives me the ice pop and I take a lick. So far so good. It tastes fine. Until I take a bite of it.

"Eh, Sean, what is that hard chewy bit inside your ice pop?" I ask as I start to pick it out of my tooth.

"A raisin."

"WHAT????!!!"

"Yeah, did you bite into my other surprise yet?" he says.

"Geeze, man-- I'm afraid to take another bite!" I answer.

Sean's like that, you know. He's a real practical joker. Oh, and for the record, he had

Ouch! I think that thing just chipped my tooth!

little bits of chocolate frozen in the center too, a little further down.

Actually, when you think about it, he's a sort of kitchen genius, or maybe I should say freezer genius. He explained that to get it right and to keep the chocolate in the middle and totally hidden he had to freeze the pops in three stages. He said the raisin went in first. The chocolate was an after thought. He just threw the raisin in to be funny, but thought the chocolate might be good. Personally, I'm not one for mixing orange juice with chocolate, but I have to give him points for creativity. Still, I'm hoping that my aunt does the baking for the sale. I mean, our team has to make **some** money, right?

Anyway, where was I? Oh, yes. The bake sale idea.

I was delighted about it because I had been working for months on the perfect birthday cake and I just knew this was going to be a great place to try my new recipe out. I was sure EVERYONE in town would be out in front of Cogan's. The tables were going to line all of Main Street up to Mitchell's.

Sean cast me a glance during training when the coach made his announcement. He sort of smiled at me. I think Sean knew what I was thinking all right, *and it wasn't about frozen orange raisin pops with chocolate.* This was just the thing I needed to show everybody in Miltown how serious I really was about proving myself.

I had exactly two weeks to come up with, finesse, and display my best cake.

I knew this was going to be a tall order because Mum and I had already tried chocolate cake and yellow cake and both times we struggled to get a cake that was light and moist and not too rich. But I was really learning how to bake so I knew that with the right recipe I could blow everyone in town away.

I started by looking on the internet and in cook books for best recipes. I liked reading the comments people made about a recipe someone posted.

Sometimes people would get pretty critical of the recipe but most times the commentators were a friendly bunch that said nice things. Mum and I figured out after a while that the best commentators were the ones who made suggestions about how to improve it.

Well, for the bake sale I was dead set on making a cake, but what kind of cake I wasn't too sure.

I thought that adding a bit of fruit into the cake batter might make it moister because any cake Mum and I made with the gluten-free flour seemed dry and crumbly in comparison to the cake I ate at Derm's party.

117

We baked a lot of practice cakes together. Dad said, "At the rate you're going, I'd have celebrated my birthday 100 times before the bake sale." Mum said a man who licks his plate and hides the leftover cake behind a frozen bag of asparagus has no room to complain.

And by the way, these were my REJECT recipes he was hiding.

Mum was awful patient with me while we practiced each night. Dessie was practically kissing my feet. Dessie has a wicked sweet tooth. Mum is forever hiding sweets because he is forever eating them until they're gone. So a free and easy slice of cake every night was a ticket to heaven for Dessie.

After a few tries I decided honey was better than sugar. It made the cake more moist and yummy, and according to Nana it's much better for you. Then I thought, wouldn't it be funny if I put a surprise ingredient in my cake? Ha! you are thinking either raisins or chocolate, right? Wouldn't you like to know! You could be close. I could hide it in there and no one would know, or would they?

I called over to Derm's house and asked him what he thought. about a honey cake with raisins and carrots in it. He said it gave him the visual of me puking on the side of the road that night on his 6th birthday. Well, I told him that I thought he might like it, and asked if he would at least sample my recipe before the bake sale.

Derm didn't say much for a minute. That's when I knew he was up to something. And I was right. He bent down and grabbed his boots.

"On one condition," he said.

"What?"

"As long as you help me stack the turf tonight."

This is Derm's turf cabin. You need to keep the turf dry or it makes a very smokey fire. That's why you can't just leave it out in the yard or on a trailer. It rains A LOT in Ireland.

I told him we were on! Then I saw the pile. I shouldn't have agreed so soon. He had tricked me! Derm had me stacking for two whole hours. That was one HUGE pile of turf!

"You only have one fireplace. What do you need all this for?" I asked him half way through.

"Oil heat is more expensive." he said. "We like to save money in the winter. We use the stove too."

All I can tell you is that after all that work I slept like a rock that night. But before I fell asleep I thought a lot about my cake.

By the end of the week I knew I was on to something. I looked at regular recipe books that used wheat. There were plenty of carrot cake recipes around. Being a science kid, I was really interested in the chemistry of cooking. I decided to study a bit on the different kinds of fats. I had to figure out which kind would make my cake taste the best: liquid vegetable oil, palm oil, butter, coconut oil, there were so many to choose from. I got Nana's help in the fat department. We decided to use a liquid oil.

Well, since this was a bake sale and there are folks in my town who can't eat dairy I thought I would try to make the cake without any milk or butter, just in case.

I wanted as many buyers as possible. My goal was to be the first to get sold out on the day of the sale.

So I got out my pencil and some paper and decided to make an original, one of a kind, gluten-free carrot cake that Granddad would prefer over the goodie, and Dad would DEFINITELY hide behind the frozen asparagus any day of the week.

I bet you are wondering what Derm and the lads thought of my final masterpiece. Well, you will have to either keep on wondering or turn the page!

Chapter 13

CHA-CHING AND ANOTHER THING....

Mum and I arrived early on the day of the bake sale. We took the far booth for our team. I figured it was the best bet because it was right on the cross between Main Street and the road to Spanish Point. The sky put out a lashing the night before but the rain had dried up and the day promised sun. I figured this would be good for profits.

We brought two carrot cakes and a tin of carrot muffins with us and set them down next to Derm's brown bread and soda bread loaves. And as the morning wore on more and more donations were piling

That's my cousin Sean standing behind me. He's collecting all the money because he's tops in math in our class. Our teacher plays around the world math facts and he always wins every round.

up. Then Sean showed up with a banner for the main bake sale.

When I saw him I said, "Glad to see you put your talents where they belong, Sean." I was just 'having him on' as the Irish like to put it. That means I was just teasing him a little bit for the fun of it.

"Well, you took all my raisins last night with all your mistakes. I couldn't make my fancy recipe," he said back in a typical Miltown-style response. We are always kidding each other like that around here.

Dessie came with us, of course. Nana had given him a handful of coins and told him to make himself happy. Don't you know that was exactly what he intended. Dessie is forever trying to make me feel bad about not being able to eat wheat or gluten. He used to love to stuff his face in front of me every chance he got and give me a detailed description of how good it tastes. Sometimes he still does that. I have even seen him eat stuff he doesn't like that much just to get my goat.

Brothers....so typical.

Someone should tell him that the taste really doesn't matter anymore to a kid with allergies. When you know you are going to end up with a list of possible problems afterward you don't want it. Hm, let's see, what would I prefer?

a. *a really nasty headache,*

b. *diarrhea afterward like I did at Doc's,*

c. *throw up all over the street in front of my friends' houses....*

So as you probably figured out, I usually just ignore Dessie when he is being obnoxious about food. After all, he is a little brother and let's face it, he just doesn't get it. Although I have to be completely honest, there have been times when I've 'lost the plot' so to

speak and have clobbered him because I just couldn't take it anymore. But it has been ages since that has happened. Mum says it's because Dessie's getting older and more mature. Dad says it's because he knows I'm tougher and has learned not to mess with me. I like Dad's way of looking at it better but I suppose Mum is right too.

It is only natural that he would be a little jealous. I mean, Mum has a whole cabinet filled with food that only I'm allowed to eat. Dessie can't touch it without asking first. If I saved every wrapper that he has stolen and eaten while hiding from us I could fill the back of Dad's trailer. There would be no room for the cows in there. So I guess that's where he gets it from.

Well, I've forgotten my story again. So sorry about that. But before I go back to the bake sale I just have to tell you the three weirdest places Mum and I have found empty wrappers:

1. Behind the freezer (I mean, HOW does he put it there without actually moving the freezer?)
2. Stuffed behind the radiator rods (Okay, I hope he was doing that in the summer because they get pretty hot.)

3. *Inside his pillow case (Okay, who wants to sleep with crinkly wrappers under their head?)*

Okay, enough of that. Let's get back to the bake sale now. Where was I? Oh yes, I left you with the image of Dessie running off to get his gluten fix with a handful of coins in his pocket.

We opened up at half-nine which is really the same as saying 9:30. There were many cars coming through town on their way to Lehinch, Spanish Point, and Quilty. I worked the street taking orders. Sean took the money while Derm and Mom bagged the baked goods. We carried on like this until about noon. I noticed that we only had one slice of gluten-free cake left, and just for the record, there were TONS of slices of soda bread still on the table.

That's when it happened. I have the moment etched in my brain like a movie scene. A lady with long red, curly hair and loads of jewelry on walked up to Mum and asked us who had made the lovely carrot cakes. Mum pointed my way and said, "T'was himself."

She gave Mum an odd glance then threw me a huge smile. "Wouldn't you know?!"

I grinned, not sure what to think of it all.

"Well, hello young man. Is this your Mum?"

"Yes."

"Great. Well, I'm Claire Conway and I'm sorry, I didn't catch your name?"

"Cilie. I'm Cilie Yack."

"And you're a footballer who bakes?"

"Yes."

"Well, I am the daughter of a hotel owner in Limerick. Have you ever heard of Niall Lynch?"

Mum threw back her head and her eyes got real wide. "I have!" she said.

Later Mum told me that the Lynch family was famous in the west of Ireland because they had a few fancy hotels where all the tourists liked to stay. There were always little reports on the news about them.

Well, I won't go into all the dirty details about that first meeting. Although I can because I have it all memorized in my head. I've even memorized how Derm blurted out to her, "This cake is actually gluten-free and it's still really good, can you believe it?"

But anyway, that wasn't what mattered to her initially. You see, her father was revamping their hotel restaurant menu in Limerick City and they had just hosted a contest among professional Irish chefs.

There is a problem though. Her father is quite particular about his desserts and he just wasn't happy with the results of the contest. After two days he hadn't picked a winner yet.

So this is where I come into the picture. Claire offered to give us a complimentary lunch the following day if we would bake another one of my 'prize worthy cakes.' Those were her words not mine, by the way. Mum said that would be grand. So I am sure you can imagine what we did that night, right?

You are exactly right....

We baked another cake!

All the chefs in the contest worked hard to please Mr. Lynch. He is a tough judge. You just don't get to be that successful without being a good critic and judge.

Chapter 14

MEETING THE MAN, MR. NIALL LYNCH

One look at Niall Lynch reminded me of the time I ran into the boiler room at my school when I was only 3 years old. Well, let me put it this way, Niall Lynch looked nothing like Mr. Finnegan. For starters he was almost completely bald in comparison. And for another thing, he dressed a lot differently than a grounds keeper does. Mr. Lynch had on a fancy suit and shiny shoes. But his face looked just like how I remembered Mr. Finnegan's did just before I ran away. Mr. Lynch had a gruff looking face. He looked like he could be mean at any minute. He seemed annoyed at just about everything.

If I could have eaten and then run off, I certainly would have. I felt the heaviness of my cake box under

Mum and Nana were so excited to have lunch at the West County. I was sweating bullets.

my feet. I wondered to myself how I would be able to talk to him.

That's when Claire Conway burst into the room. She lit up when she saw us sitting at our table. She said she was delighted that we turned up after all. She chatted a bit with Mum and Nana. Then she sent a server to take our order and another to serve us drinks. When Claire returned she asked me how I felt about meeting Mr. Lynch after the meal.

Well, I have to be honest. I'm not as tough sometimes as Dad thinks I am. I got this big lump at the bottom of my neck. I just about choked on the ice water I was about to swallow.

My eyes must have bulged because she smiled and said not to worry. Claire promised to go with me and hold the cake.

Mum said, "Well that's a relief. He's a bit cagey about it. I'm afraid he might just drop the cake after all his efforts."

Well, I don't have to tell you that Mum's comment was a bit embarrassing. I was really trying to put on a good face for myself. I sort of smiled and mumbled to Claire, "That would be grand." And then I ate my lunch.

Niall Lynch was a tough looking boss. But I have to admit he was not so gruff once I started talking to him. And by the way, he absolutely loved the cake. He carried on about it for a while. Then he even sent a few slices back to the pastry chef in the back.

Soon Mr. Lynch started talking business with me. Claire explained to him that the cake was actually gluten-free. Mr. Lynch was pleasantly surprised. He said it was healthier but still tasted as good as any other bakery cake. All their visitors would be over the moon about it, even the ones that eat wheat and gluten.

Mr. Lynch said his hotel does get guests with dietary needs. He felt this was a good opportunity to get better publicity and more visitors. He wanted to be the first hotel chain to offer guests a gluten-free cake.

Mr. Lynch asked to buy my cake recipe. That's right-- B-U-Y it. Can you believe that? Once more, he said he would give me and Mum some cooking classes, compliments of his hotel company.

Then Mr. Lynch gave me a special chef's hat and apron to keep.

"There you go Master Yack," he said with a smile. "Every sous chef needs a hat and an apron to do the job right."

Delighted I took the hat and put it on. "Thanks a million Mr. Lynch!" I said. Claire thought I looked quite handsome in it. When

I landed back at the table to say hello to Mum and Nana they were very impressed as well.

Claire then gave us a tour of the chef's kitchen. I wasn't able to see the pastry kitchen, though, because of all the wheat in there. I did get to meet the chef who would be baking my cakes for the customers. Claire said that they have a separate prep kitchen that was going to make the perfect place for their special carrot cake baking.

Dad is very proud of my efforts. He still has the issue of the Clare Champion with me on the cover posted on our fridge. Mum says that they must get a frame for it. Now everyone in town is always asking about my budding career as a sous chef.

But enough about all that.

Do you want to know the BEST part? Every time we travel passed one of Mr. Lynch's fancy hotels we always get to stop and have REAL cake, just like everyone else does.

Chapter 15

FINAL THOUGHTS AND AN INVITATION

Well, that is the story about my life. I hope you enjoyed it. I certainly had a good time telling you all about myself. And you know what? It's funny. When I first found out that I couldn't eat goodie I thought my life was over. But do you know what I learned? Giving up goodie was the best thing that ever happened to me.

Just look at how much my life has improved since then. First there is the obvious benefit of never having to poop myself again or puke all over the road. Second, I met my best friend Derm. Third, I improved my reputation at my school. Fourth, I started playing Gaelic football and I found out I wasn't so bad at it after all. **AND** best of all, I became a pretty famous sous chef in

Cilie Yack's cake sold here!
& GLUTEN-FREE

my own hometown. I am definitely no longer dosser material. Mum and Dad couldn't be more proud. Everyone around me takes notice of me now in a good way. They don't think of me as a hooligan running amuck and getting myself into trouble anymore. I don't think of myself that way either now.

By the way, my meeting with Mr. Lynch was about five months ago. Now my cakes are not only in his restaurants. They sell a couple at the bakery in Ennis now too. Mr. Lynch ships them over there and they keep them fully wrapped so no wheat crumbs can mix with them or anything. Mr Lynch says my cake has regular customers every week.

Life is great now in Miltown. Believe it or not, Mum and I do still make our cake at home from time to time. After a thing like that happens to you there are a lot of new expectations.

Derm said that I should make another recipe or two that could really put the under 10s team on the map permanently. Our manager was delighted because the Lynch family donated enough money to help us buy those lights. They came in handy last night when we played against Ennistymon. Don't you know, we won again. Derm scored the winning goal. It was a close match, but he was pretty swift at getting the ball down the field in the last couple of minutes. We only won by 2 points, but it was the finals and that made our team champions.

"You rode the wave of celebrity on your carrot cake way too long," Derm told me after the match. "We need a new victory food," he added.

"Ha!" Sean shouted. "Where's your cake box? It'll do me fine. I'm hungry!"

I laughed.

We hung out for a while at the field and then went to Cogan's for a celebration dinner. Mum brought me a

In Gaelic football players move the ball up the field three ways. They can pass it to teammates, solo it (which is dropping and then toe-kicking the ball upward into their hands), or they can kick it down the field like they do in soccer.

meal from home and of course some homemade cake. We ate every last piece and I shaved the bits off of the bottom with my fingernails. It was so good we didn't let anything go to waste.

Now all the lads want to know what I plan to do next. Chocolate cake, banana cake, pie, apple tart, they offered a long list of suggestions. Our manager joked that we need another great recipe because our field needs new stands now. Dad just laughed out loud when he heard that. I could tell he was proud.

Which brings me back to why I bothered to tell you all this stuff in the first place.

Do you want to know?

Well, I have decided to finally start a cooking club especially for kids on special diets just like me. All our recipes are going to be gluten-free, too, just like my cake. I'm calling it Cilie Yack's Sous Club for Kids. I got that idea from Mr. Lynch actually. So if you think you may want to join, come on over to my website and check it out!

www.cilie-yack.org

Oh, and one more thing- Dessie says that he thinks that brothers should be allowed to join too. I say of course! As long as you are a kid and you want to learn how to cook gluten-free recipes you are INVITED!

You don't have to have celiac to be a member. You don't have to have food allergies, either. We won't turn you away. But if you have food allergies, this club will make you feel right at home, unlike any other club you've joined or party you've ever gone to before.

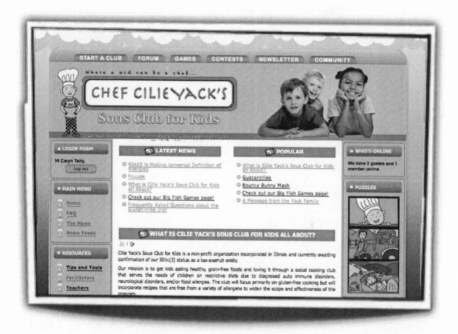

Check us out online! We are having our very first KIDS ONLY recipe contest in January 2011. We want YOU to enter. We've got games and puzzles and activities there too. I also have my very own newsletter. So if you want to hear more stories about my life come check everything out.

Try making Cilie's Famous Carrot Cake Recipe!

INGREDIENTS:
- 4 eggs (or **if you are egg-free use:** 2 tbsp Ener-G, 6 tbsp warm water, and 2 smashed bananas, which is actually about 6 eggs) *Ener-G is not corn-free*
- 3 cups of grated carrots (Be sure to grate them into large strands, as if you were adding them to a salad.)
- 2 teaspoons pure vanilla (Be sure it is corn free if you have a corn allergy, if you are not sure just omit it.)
- 3/4 cup vegetable oil
- 1/2 cup organic apple sauce (made without citric acid)
- 3/4 cup evaporated cane juice (or you can do 1/2 cup of honey instead)
- 3/4 cup organic brown sugar (corn-free)
- 1 1/3 cup white rice flour
- 1/4 cup tapioca flour
- 1/2 cup potato flour
- 2 teaspoons Hains Featherweight baking powder (It is the only one that is corn-free.)
- 2 teaspoons baking soda
- 1/2 teaspoon salt
- 2 teaspoons cinnamon

Powdered Sugar for Frosting:
Use a blender to make your own corn-free powdered sugar. Just mix all the following ingredients together in a high power blender:
- 3 cups evaporated cane juice
- 6 tablespoons (3/8 cup) of tapioca starch
- 1 teaspoon vanilla (Be sure it is corn free if you have a corn allergy, if you are not sure just omit it.)

No wheat, soy, nuts, tree nuts, dairy, corn, or gluten!

DIRECTIONS:

Preheat your oven to 350°F. In a mixer blend the eggs. or egg replacer. Add the oil, vanilla, sugars, cinnamon, and applesauce. When it is well blended add the carrots.

In a separate bowl mix all the dry ingredients and sift well. Add the dry ingredients and blend on medium-high for 1 minute.

Grease two 8-inch round cake pans. Pour half of the batter into each cake pan and spread evenly. Bake for 40 minutes. Let cool before removing from the oven. When the cake is cooled refrigerate or freeze until you are ready to serve.

Frosting:

Use up to 6 cups of palm shortening and 3 cups of powdered sugar. You may like more frosting, or you may want less. Just use a ratio of 2 parts palm shortening to 1 part sugar. The result will be a nice smooth frosting that isn't too sweet. Only spread the frosting on a well chilled cake. Frosting works best when it is spread just after mixing and then refrigerated until it is ready to serve.

Made in the USA
Lexington, KY
19 June 2013